THE FIRST THING Cleo noticed was the screams. Some were filled with anger, some were filled with terror, but all mixed together like the dying shrill of a fallen bird.

The second thing Cleo noticed was the bodies. Death surrounded her. Men, women, children, facedown in the dirt, or cold dead eyes staring unblinking at the sun, like a photograph of a frozen moment in time. The bodies were scattered across the village as if they were rice grains sprinkled to the wind by a giant hand. Cleao saw warriors race to and fro with weapons. She spotted a nearby tipi and dragged herself toward shelter.

Suddenly, a warrior raced past and accidentally kicked Cleo in the legs. "Ouch!" she yelped in protest. Cleo froze. *I felt that!* she thought. *My legs* . . .

Like a newborn fawn gingerly unfolding its legs to venture a first step, Cleo unsteadily rose from the cold dirt to stand.

"I feel everything . . . ," she whispered.

"Why did you do that?" she heard Alex's voice boom in her head. "Of all the stupid—oh my God, Cleo! You're walking!"

Book III

Red Wolf's Daughter

A novelization by
Dan Danko and Tom Mason
BASED ON A TELEPLAY BY JEFF COHEN

BANTAM BOOKS

New York · Toronto · London · Sydney · Auckland

RL 5.5, AGES 10 & UP

RED WOLF'S DAUGHTER

A Bantam Skylark Book / March 2003

ISBN: 0-553-48761-2 (pbk.)
0-553-13022-6 (lib. bdg.)

Visit us on the Web! www.randomhouse.com/kids

Educators and librarians, for a variety of teaching tools, visit
us at www.randomhouse.com/teachers

Published simultaneously in the United States and Canada

Bantam Skylark is an imprint of Random House Children's
Books, a division of Random House, Inc. SKYLARK BOOK
and colophon and BANTAM BOOKS and colophon are
registered trademarks of Random House, Inc.

PRINTED IN THE UNITED STATES OF AMERICA

OPM 10 9 8 7 6 5 4 3 2 1

BOOK III

Red Wolf's Daughter

Prologue

A blackness moved through the still waters of the lake. To the casual eye, the amorphous mass and the water were one. It had no shape, no form, but most certainly a purpose. It rose from the murky depths like an ancient turtle gently floating to the surface for a new gulp of air. As the blackness rose, its vagueness found definition, and a shape was carved from the surrounding water—the shape of a woman.

She burst from the lake and rose into the air. The unsettled waters of Walloha lapped at her bare feet. She walked on its surface as easily as she might stroll on grass in a park on a sunny afternoon, and she made her way to the pebbled shore.

Her long, gray hair rested on her noble shoulders. Her skin was tan and her brown eyes burned with the eternal knowledge of her immortality. She was the spirit of the lake. She was Walloha.

She left the lake behind and set foot on land. Cries of war immediately greeted her.

The Nez Perce had lived on the shores of Walloha since their earliest history, and they had been at war with the Blackfoot for almost as long. As in any war that extends for generations, there had been great casualties on both sides, but recently the Blackfoot had gained the upper hand and the Nez Perce numbers diminished in the face of death. Today, the fight had been brought to the Nez Perce village where the last of the noble people lived.

Blackfoot warriors attacked the Nez Perce tribe like locusts descending on a field of swaying crops. Their clubs and tomahawks cut and pounded their enemies with a zealous disregard for life. Arrows sliced through the air and found their deadly marks. Blood stained the soil, and the earth ran red with death.

The Nez Perce tried to fight back, but the Blackfoot's numbers were greater, their warriors younger and strong. Nez Perce women defended their wounded men as best they could, while their children cowered in fear, crying out for the nightmare to end.

Walloha walked through the battle, invisible to its combatants. If she could have cried, she would have. The violence and the hatred of this place were stronger than her power, and Walloha shuddered with the children as she passed through the carnage.

A Blackfoot warrior ran down a Nez Perce warrior and leveled him with a single blow. Another Nez Perce warrior fired two quick shots with his bow and didn't miss with either. A young Blackfoot, barely fifteen, screamed to the gods and flung his tomahawk at an opponent.

Walloha made her way across the Nez Perce village to a tree-encircled clearing just outside the battle zone.

"Eagle!" Walloha cried to the clear blue sky. "I need to speak with you! White Buffalo! Badger! Quickly!"

From the land and the sky around Walloha, three figures appeared in a flash—faster than the human eye could follow. They seemed human, but different somehow. The one called Eagle perched in a tree above Walloha. His red eyes looked down upon her. His skin was whitish and his chest was bare and strong. His nose was broad and curved, coming to a sharp end, seemingly more beak in appearance than nose.

From the bushes rose Badger. She appeared to be younger than Walloha, less serene, as she paced around the river god. She was covered in spiky brown fur, and even her long hair stood on end. Her small, beady eyes darted about with nervous tension.

Finally came White Buffalo. He stepped solemnly into the clearing. His large frame caused Badger to scuffle back toward the bush for a moment. He, too, was covered in fur, although it was soft and woolly. His features were chiseled and wise, appearing as old as the Earth itself. His hands were thick and, if he were so inclined, could snap Badger's neck like a toothpick.

Badger wiggled her nose and sniffed at the air.

"This village is the last of the Nez Perce

people," Walloha told her fellow spirits. "If the fighting doesn't stop, they'll all be gone."

"But what can we do?" Badger asked, her voice soaked with worry.

"Blackfoot are warriors. It's their way." Eagle offered this stern explanation.

"The war between them is old, hard to stop." The thought certainly saddened Buffalo, but he too was unsure of any solutions.

"But there may still be a way for peace," Walloha countered.

"How, Walloha?" Buffalo asked.

"Give me your consent to find a sacrifice."

The group fell silent, and in their hushed moment, the violent screams of war cut into their circle, a dreadful reminder of the crisis. Finally, Eagle raised his head.

"It must be one who is willing to make the sacrifice," he stated.

"Yes," Walloha agreed. "It's the only way."

White Buffalo and Badger nodded and disappeared into the bush. Eagle nodded as well, then took to the sky. Now more bird than man, he floated into the heavens with the majestic grace of an ancient spirit.

Chapter One

Cleo Bellows rolled her wheelchair through the crowded cafeteria. She cut left around one girl, then grabbed the right wheel of her chair and twisted around a boy who bolted out from nowhere. She was almost in the clear when a lanky boy turned from the lunch line and nearly doubled over Cleo's lap. He teetered to the left and grabbed his milk, but sacrificed his chocolate cake. It fell to the ground, icing down, of course.

"What're you, blind?" David grumbled at Cleo, examining the tragedy that had once been his tasty dessert.

"Who said that?" Cleo asked, reaching her hands out, searching the air.

David leaned over and picked up his cake off the ground. Dirt and hair were stuck to the frosting.

"So what am I going to do about dessert?" David asked.

"What? What?" Cleo cupped her hand to her ear, pretending to be deaf. She slowly rolled away, one hand still nestled against her lobe. "Was someone there? Hello? Anybody?"

David watched Cleo roll away. He certainly loved chocolate cake, but he smiled. Cleo wasn't so bad on the eyes.

"Dear Dad." Cleo typed the two words into a new e-mail, then stopped. She stared at them and for a moment wondered why she had typed them at all. How long had her father been missing? Long enough for Cleo to have trouble remembering his face or the sound of his voice. She didn't forget often, but when she did, a chill raced down her spine.

Cleo rested her chin in her hand and collected her thoughts. Her brown hair hung down the side of her face and covered her long, artistic fingers. Emotions swirled behind brown eyes, and she immediately went back to typing to fight back tears. Sitting in her father's den, working on his computer, made her feel closer to her dad—and more far away.

"Things are starting to get really complicated. Mom says I should get out more, be like other kids, but what she doesn't get is that I like hanging out by myself."

Cleo stopped again. She lightly tapped the keys, taking a moment to plot her course.

"You always got that about me." She continued typing. "I still miss your bedtime stories, even though I'm way too old for them. And I won't stop looking for you until I can hear them again. I know you're not going to receive this, but, love forever. Cleo."

She finished her e-mail, quickly addressed it to "DAD@WHO_AM_I_KIDDING.COM," read over it a final time, then hit Delete. The message instantly disappeared, with no trace that it had ever existed—just like her father.

Cleo stared at the large plasma screen mounted to the wall. Before she had decided to type her e-mail, she had been wandering up and down the various corridors of the Cyber-Museum, searching for clues, but mostly killing time until her brother, Alex, got home. Her father had entered digital scans of hundreds of artifacts into the computer and stored them here, in a virtual museum. She picked up her search where she had left off: the Plains Indians room.

Cleo was certainly frustrated. She was one of the top students at her school, so why couldn't she find anything in the CyberMuseum that would help her locate her father? She ran her fingers through her hair and sighed.

One thing she and Alex knew for certain: Something amazing had happened to the Cyber-Museum that made it a portal into myths. By touching an artifact from any era, she or Alex, or anyone, could travel into a myth and assume the role of one of its key players. Alex had already been Theseus and battled the Minotaur, and Vali, the son of the Norse god Loki. The adventures were real and sometimes all too dangerous.

That was what must have happened to their father. He had, probably unwittingly, gotten lost in a myth. He had touched something in the CyberMuseum that began his adventure, and if Cleo and Alex could just find that artifact and touch it as well, they could find their missing father and bring him back to the real world. Easier said than done.

Thousands of artifacts filled the halls and rooms of the CyberMuseum. It was worse than trying to find a needle in a haystack. *At least a needle will poke you to let you know it's there,* Cleo thought.

Several Plains Indians artifacts were displayed on the screen before her: a club, a pipe, some arrowheads, a pair of moccasins, and a few other items.

Cleo rolled out from behind the desk and toward the screen. She lifted her hand, her fingers cautiously extending to the beckoning plasma screen.

"Cleo." Alex's stern voice sounded from behind her.

"What?" Cleo replied, retracting her hand, trying to cover her aching temptation.

"Nothing," Alex said, and entered their father's study. "Just get away from the screen, okay?"

"Why?" Cleo's voice was hard, but Alex didn't seem to notice his sister's anger.

"Because . . . it's on."

"I turned it on."

"I thought we had an understanding," Alex said. "We don't turn it on until just before I go in."

Cleo gave Alex a long look. "That's the thing."

"What's the thing?"

"It's not about us, Alex. It's about you," Cleo protested. "*You* look for Dad and *I* just sit around watching. Just 'cause you're the guy, the big hero, you get to do it and I don't."

"No, you stay here because you're in—" Alex caught himself, refusing to allow his anger to speak for him. "Cleo . . ."

"Like you can take it and I can't?" Cleo shot back.

"Look, this is not some video game. It's real!" Alex knew he didn't have to remind his sister that the myths they entered were as real as any day at school—only a hundred times more dangerous. And that there was no room for a wheelchair in the danger he faced.

Cleo glared at Alex but slowly rolled back a few feet from the plasma screen. She watched her older brother kneel and tighten the laces on his running shoes.

"Are those Plains Indians artifacts?" Alex asked, cutting the silence.

"Pretty obvious, isn't it?" Cleo's tone was surly. "Why're you tightening your shoes? You know you can't take anything with you."

"Helps psych me up."

"Uh-huh." Cleo wasn't really interested in the answer. She rolled to her father's desk and pulled off a book. When Alex stood, she tossed the volume to him.

"Heroines in the Myst of Time," Alex read from the cover. "Let me guess, chock-full of female heroes battling dragons and ne'er-do-wells? What's your point?"

"He's my father too."

"Yeah? But they didn't have sidewalk ramps in the mists of time."

"They didn't have sidewalks!" Cleo spat back. "So what's the problem?"

"I don't go in with my running shoes; you don't go in with your chair!" Alex countered. "How's that for a problem?"

Cleo couldn't debate Alex's logic. She didn't want to. She only wanted to help find her father. If she thought about it for too long, she'd never do what she needed to do. If she took her time and planned where to go and what to touch on the screen, Alex would figure out what she was up to and stop her.

"See ya," Cleo offered, and slapped one of the artifacts on the plasma screen.

"Cleo!" Alex screamed, but it was too late. There was no sound, and worse yet, no Cleo. Her empty wheelchair stood as the lone reminder she had ever been there at all.

Chapter Two

The first thing Cleo noticed was the screams. Some were filled with anger, some were filled with terror, but all mixed together like the dying shrill of a fallen bird.

The second thing Cleo noticed was the bodies. Death surrounded her. Men, women, children, facedown in the dirt, or cold dead eyes staring unblinking at the sun, like a photograph of a frozen moment in time. The bodies were scattered across the village as if they were rice grains sprinkled to the wind by a giant hand. Cleo saw warriors race to and fro with weapons. She spotted a nearby tipi and dragged herself toward shelter.

Suddenly, a warrior raced past and accidentally kicked Cleo in the legs. "Ouch!" she yelped in protest. Cleo froze. *I felt that!* she thought. *My legs . . .*

Like a newborn fawn gingerly unfolding its legs to venture a first step, Cleo unsteadily rose from the cold dirt to stand.

"I feel everything . . . ," she whispered.

"Why did you do that?" she heard Alex's voice boom in her head. "Of all the stupid—oh my God, Cleo! You're walking!"

Before Cleo could answer, she spotted a Nez Perce boy, no older than she was, running in her direction. Cleo wasn't sure whether the boy was running *to* her or *away* from something, but her answer came in the downward swing of a Blackfoot club. The boy crumpled to the earth like a house of cards.

Cleo gasped in shock and the Blackfoot warrior turned toward her. He raised his club, its end now freshly red with the blood of his victim, and charged Cleo.

"Run, Cleo!" Alex screamed in her head. This was the first time, and in Alex's mind the last, he was left in the study to watch the adventure while Cleo entered a myth. He knew from Cleo's experience that he'd be able to watch everything she did on the plasma screen and speak to her. Only Cleo would be able to hear his voice while she was in the myth. Not being able to help as his sister was chased by an enraged Plains warrior seemed far worse than dealing with the reality and fear of any myth he entered.

Cleo ran, but her legs, unused for the past four years, were unsure. The Blackfoot was on top of her before she could think of defending herself. A war cry exploded from the Blackfoot's lungs. He raised his weapon over his head.

A Nez Perce warrior blindsided the Blackfoot warrior and upended him with his spear. "Run!" the Nez Perce warrior urged Cleo.

She raced behind the tipi and watched the warrior raise his spear above his head to strike the fallen Blackfoot. But as the Nez Perce fighter had surprised the Blackfoot warrior, he in turn was surprised by the spear that struck his arm.

"Strong Bear!" she heard another Nez Perce cry out in alarm at the sight of her wounded defender.

Strong Bear spun to face the leader of the

Blackfoot, Bloody Chief. The two warriors stared each other down. Strong Bear appeared to be in his prime as a fighter, his long black hair braided behind his head. And Bloody Chief was at least fifteen years older; an aura of power clung to him. He looked fresh to the fight though he must have been battling for just as long as the younger man.

The two men charged. While they fought, the fallen Blackfoot rose to his feet and spotted Cleo behind the tipi. She fled, the angry Blackfoot hot on her heels.

"Seeloo!" a voice cried out.

A powerful man, even older than Bloody Chief, fell upon the Blackfoot warrior. This was Red Wolf, chief of the Nez Perce people. A few proud eagle feathers hung from his graying hair. While ferocity raged in Bloody Chief's eyes, wisdom filled Red Wolf's. But he was not just a man of thought; he was also a man of war. Red Wolf's huge war club cracked across the Blackfoot warrior's head. The club was a dark red wood, and one side was studded with jagged wolf's teeth. It was more than two feet long and its head was carved into the shape of a fierce wolf. Few opponents saw Red Wolf's club and lived to tell the tale. Cleo never looked back to see what happened, but she could tell by the sound, a horrible wet thunk, that the Blackfoot would never chase anyone again.

Cleo's legs finally gave their full cooperation and she raced from the village. She found a small clearing, far enough away that even the sounds of battle had trouble finding her. She fell to her knees, her heart pounding against her chest and her breath shallow and rapid like a frightened rabbit.

But her peace was momentary. From behind Cleo, a hand reached out and grabbed her shoulder.

Chapter Three

"It's all right now."

Cleo spun in the dirt and faced Walloha. In this stranger's eyes, Cleo saw shelter from the violent insanity. She melted into Walloha's arms with the same explosion of relief she would've felt if she had been reunited with her own missing father.

"So, is this the one?" Eagle asked, suddenly appearing in a nearby tree. His human feet acted like talons and gripped the thick branch.

"Seems awful skinny for a sacrifice," Badger commented, showing herself in the bush. She nervously twitched her girlish nose. The fur on her back stood erect as she looked Cleo over.

Cleo wasn't sure how to take these creatures. They talked like humans, yet, like Walloha, they were so much more. She felt a great energy coming from the creatures, a vibrancy that regular humans did not have.

"Without her, we can't save the tribe," Walloha reminded them.

"And if she won't do it?" Eagle countered.

"We're lost, too! Without their prayers to us . . ." White Buffalo finally appeared to show his support. His massive hands betrayed their strength and gently touched Cleo's chin.

"Their memories of us . . . ," Badger added, knowing how important these tribes were to their existence.

"Their stories about us, their songs, their art . . . Without them, we will disappear." White Buffalo's lead words sank in the air.

"No them, no us," Badger said.

"We have to decide," Walloha said, petting Cleo's hair.

"She'll do fine," White Buffalo agreed, then lumbered into the mist that had appeared behind him.

"Yes. I accept." Eagle then disappeared as quickly as he had arrived. Cleo heard a noise, then saw a great bird lift into a misty cloud.

"Okay. Me too," Badger said, then faded back into the brush.

"I don't understand," Cleo said to Walloha. She had suddenly become frightened again. She wondered whether the four spirits meant to cause her harm.

"In here you understand," Walloha said, touching Cleo's chest over her beating heart. "Your heart shall tell you everything you need to know."

Walloha released Cleo and stood. She smiled at Cleo and added, "Pray to the lake, Seeloo," then slowly faded like an enigmatic dream retreating before the dawn.

"What the heck was that about?" Alex asked.

"I don't know."

"Something about a sacrifice?" Alex had seen Walloha and the three other spirits on the plasma screen, but he was just as lost as Cleo.

"I think so." Cleo's voice was unsteady.

"You okay?" Alex asked.

"Some of them were just boys," Cleo said. The violent images still stung her mind, but she knew she had to return to the village.

"I saw," Alex said, not knowing how to re-assure Cleo.

Cleo crept up behind a tipi. Bloody Chief stood in the center of the carnage. "Enough!" he shouted. The battle was over. "We'll take the spoils tomorrow."

A young man dressed in battle gear almost as elaborate as Bloody Chief's embraced the chief in a fit of victory.

"This victory shall be remembered forever, Father!" he cried out.

"Tlesca, my son, today is a great day for our people," Bloody Chief answered.

With a victory cry from Tlesca, the Blackfoot warriors retreated from the village, leaving in their wake the decimated population of the Nez Perce people.

"So who am I and where am I?" Cleo asked as she finally came out of hiding and rushed to help the injured villagers.

"I don't know. I don't have enough to go on," she heard Alex reply.

"Seeloo!" a voice cried out from across the village.

"That's me," Cleo said to Alex.

"I got that much down," Alex snorted back.

Cleo turned to see Red Wolf helping the injured Strong Bear to a tipi.

"I'm needed," Cleo said, and rushed into the tipi after Red Wolf.

"Hurry! He's losing blood" was the command that greeted her the moment she entered. Red Wolf knelt over Strong Bear, applying a balm to the bloody wound on his left side.

Red Wolf thrust a piece of leather into Cleo's hands and shifted to the side so she could tend to the wounded warrior. Cleo froze.

"Tourniquet," Alex prompted in her head.

"Right . . . ," Cleo muttered under her breath. She closed her eyes for a moment and retrieved all the information she'd learned in the first-aid health class she'd had to take two semesters ago. *Never thought I'd use that stuff,* she thought as she prepared the leather strips.

Cleo did her best to ignore the blood flowing onto her hands and wrapped the leather strip around the wound.

"You've got the gift of medicine, like your father," Strong Bear said, then winced from the pain.

"She's learning," Red Wolf said, admiring his daughter's work.

Cleo moved so that Red Wolf could assume

the primary spot over Strong Bear. Red Wolf produced a buffalo bladder filled with lake water, roots, florets, and various natural items whose origins Cleo could only guess at.

"I failed my chief," Strong Bear groaned.

"You saved my daughter's life," Red Wolf corrected.

The words hit Cleo. This was her father—or, rather, Seeloo's father? She was the chief's daughter! *Very cool,* Cleo mused.

"Tomorrow will be better." Strong Bear mustered what little strength he had and tried to rise onto his hands. Red Wolf gently guided his brave warrior back to the ground.

"You won't be fighting, Strong Bear."

"I have to." Strong Bear was a fierce warrior and a proud Nez Perce. He would not give up until he had no life left in his body.

"You're wounded." Red Wolf scooped a handful of the salve from the buffalo bladder and pressed it into Strong Bear's wound.

"But . . ." Strong Bear winced.

"It's over." Red Wolf's bitter words stung his tongue. "Too many of them. Too few of us."

A silence passed between the two men, then Red Wolf turned to Cleo. "Get more snowberry," he said, handing her the bladder. "As much as you can."

"Snowberry?" Alex said. "Sounds like a breakfast cereal."

Cleo knew it wasn't a cereal, but beyond that, snowberry might as well have been kryptonite. She nodded to Red Wolf and rose to exit the tipi.

"And be careful," he warned. "There may still be Blackfoot on this side of the lake. Don't wander too far."

Cleo left the safety of Red Wolf behind and rushed into an unsure world, one filled with the death cries of Indian warriors eager to spill her blood onto the cold earth.

Chapter Four

Cleo raced through the brush, more enthusiastic to test the limitations of her legs than to find the mysterious snowberry Red Wolf had requested.

"Alex?"

"I'm here," she heard him respond.

"It's like one of those miracle cures you see on TV, but you know it can't be true," Cleo enthused, jumping to the top of a boulder and then back down the other side just to show the world and herself that she could.

She felt giddy, almost weightless. She had never given up hope that she would be able to walk again, but for it actually to happen, for her to be running and jumping and kicking . . . it was beyond her wildest expectations. She stopped suddenly.

"You think I'll be able to walk when I get back?" She already knew the answer, but she was hoping Alex could convince her otherwise.

"I wouldn't count on it, Cleo" was all he said.

Cleo noticed a bush that looked like the one Red Wolf had crushed into the bladder. "Snowberry . . . ," she said, and began picking florets.

"I'm sorry," Alex finally said. He didn't want to shatter Cleo's fantasy, but someone had to be the voice of reason.

"Okay, so my father's Red Wolf." Cleo ignored Alex's sentiment. She filled the bladder and turned back to the village. "We're Nez Perce Indians . . ."

"So you're probably somewhere in what's now Montana or Idaho, and you're losing a war with the Blackfoot." Alex was just as eager to change the subject and gladly shifted to Cleo's myth conundrum. "The Nez Perce were famous for breeding Appaloosas, but I don't see horses, so this has gotta be before the Europeans got there."

"The Europeans?" Cleo asked.

"Yeah. A lot of people don't know it, but there were no horses in the Americas until the Europeans arrived in the sixteenth century. That was when the first horses were used by Native Americans."

"Glad to know the Europeans brought something other than smallpox," Cleo commented. "What about Seeloo? Any leads?"

"I'm all over the Net. Nothing. Not a single reference to Seeloo." Alex thought for a moment, then added, "I'm gonna call Max Asher. He'll know about this stuff."

Max was their father's mentor, and Cleo knew that if anyone could tell them who Seeloo was, it would be him.

While Alex dialed Max, Cleo reentered the Nez Perce village. The scene was sadly the same. The living mourned for the dead. A lone voice floated into the sky like the notes of a gentle flute. It chanted of death and sorrow.

Cleo followed the haunting lamentation and came upon a mother cradling her dead son, barely older than Cleo. The mother laid her son's lifeless body on the ground, pulled out a rough knife, and cut her hair. The knife's coarse edge, carved from the bones of a dead buffalo, bit into the woman's gray hairs. The intensity of her chant grew with the unabated flow of her tears.

Cleo saw Red Wolf speaking with the handful of surviving warriors capable of fighting. He praised their bravery and effort and bid them courage and strength for tomorrow. Even Strong Bear stood among them, refusing to lie idle. Cleo was amazed by the bravery of these people, even though defeat seemed unavoidable.

Chapter Five

Night fell, but with it came no sleep. After hours of walking among the wounded, Cleo and Red Wolf had used the last of the snowberry. Now the two walked quietly along the solemn shores of Lake Walloha.

"Tomorrow, one more battle," Red Wolf stated. "I'll face Bloody Chief. If I can kill him, I'll die content."

"We should get out of here," Cleo immediately replied.

Red Wolf stopped walking. His stern eyes locked onto Cleo. "You want us to run?"

"What choice do we have?" Cleo reasoned.

"They'd only run faster, pick us off, and cause us more shame." Red Wolf didn't try to hide his anger at Cleo's suggestion. The very thought disgusted him. "You know that."

"What happens to the people if they lose you?"

"If?" Red Wolf held Cleo by the shoulders and looked unblinking into her eyes. "You *are* going to lose me," he said.

Red Wolf looked down at his daughter. He pulled Cleo closer and touched her cheek with the back of his hand. Cleo closed her eyes and pretended her own father was reassuring her, touching her face to say "It will be okay." She felt great sorrow. Though she was not Seeloo, the thought of losing a second father was almost more than she could bear.

"Once I am gone, the Blackfoot will kill the survivors or take them as slaves," Red Wolf warned her. "Promise me, no matter what happens, you will show them a brave face."

Cleo gave a solemn nod, then looked out to Lake Walloha. "What does it mean to pray to the lake?"

"Who told you to do that?" Red Wolf's concern took Cleo by surprise.

"I just . . . heard it."

"It's true, good things come up from under the water, but be careful what you say to Walloha," Red Wolf cautioned, shaking his head. "Spirits . . . they always want something."

Red Wolf walked into the darkness, leaving Cleo to stand alone at the lake's lapping shore. The full moon hung in the sky like a watchful eye staring down on Cleo's every move. She knelt near the lake's edge and carefully looked into its dark, murky waters. What peered back was not Cleo's own pretty face, but that of a beautiful young Native American girl the same age as Cleo. Her eyes were dark, as was her long braided hair.

So this is me, Cleo thought. *So this is Seeloo.*

Cleo stood. Red Wolf was nowhere to be seen. Nearby, the fires of the Nez Perce village cut through the night with their dancing flames.

"Alex?"

"Yeah?"

"I don't know if Dad's been here at all," Cleo confessed. "Maybe this wasn't such a good idea. I don't feel him."

"There are thousands of myths, Cleo. Dad can't be in all of them." Alex tried to reassure her, but Cleo didn't respond. After a few moments of silence, he added, "Find the way to come back." If

Cleo could find the object she had touched on the plasma screen that had sent her into the myth, she should be able to get back home.

Cleo kicked the pebbles at her feet. Her heart grew heavy at the thought of returning. Not just because she would lose the use of her legs, but because she had failed to find her father.

With a final look into the waters of Walloha, Cleo headed back toward the village. As she passed a tree, she brushed one of the branches that extended over the path. The dew hanging delicately from the pine needles shuddered from the impact and fell to the ground.

As the drop of water plummeted, it grew. Cleo didn't see, but Alex, alertly watching the whole scene on the plasma screen, did.

"Heads up," he warned Cleo. "I think she's back."

Cleo turned in time to see that she was indeed back. The drop had grown to the size of a woman, and it began to take that same shape. Walloha materialized before Cleo's eyes.

"You're . . . Walloha?" Cleo asked, almost afraid to hear the answer.

Walloha's only reply was to touch Cleo's cheek and smile. Once again, Cleo felt warm, safe.

"The spirit of the lake . . ."

"I'm here," Walloha said. "Tell me what you want."

"To stop the killing." The words came out of Cleo's mouth before she could even form the thought. Cleo wanted, more than to find her father or to get home, an end to the madness that she had witnessed.

"Peace is costly," Walloha warned.

"How costly?"

Walloha stopped, not to consider the answer, but to give Cleo time to think of what she was asking. "To save your people? Your life."

"That's why I'm here?" Cleo asked.

"Yes."

"I don't understand. Do I have a choice?" Cleo's voice was twisted by both frustration and fear.

"You'll make the right one," Walloha answered, and walked toward the water.

"Wait . . . please . . ." Cleo's words fell on deaf ears as Walloha dove beneath the waters and disappeared.

"Max isn't in his office. I just left a message," Cleo heard Alex say. "There is no way I'm gonna let you be sacrificed!"

"I don't think this is up to you, Alex."

"So who is it up to? Some watery Froot Loop?"

"No," Cleo replied. "It's up to me. I can save the Nez Perce."

Before the final words left her mouth, she stopped paying attention to what Alex was saying. She stared out across the calm waters of Lake Walloha. On the other shore, like small cat eyes peering out from a bush at midnight, the fires of the Blackfoot dotted the landscape.

"I'm gonna talk to those people."

"Those people? In case you forgot, those people were running through your village with axes six hours ago! No way! You're gonna sit right there until I get back," Alex commanded. "I'm gonna go find Max."

Cleo didn't know Alex immediately raced out of the study to find Max, and she probably wouldn't have cared. Finding a solution was her only concern. She dragged a nearby canoe across the shore, pebbles cutting into its belly. With a final push, the canoe touched the waters of Walloha and became nearly weightless. Cleo climbed inside. Her paddle slapped against the placid face of the lake and pushed her toward the waiting Blackfoot. High above, the moon cut through the darkness, a lonesome and silent witness to the fate that Cleo had bravely chosen to embrace.

Chapter Six

The head of the canoe scraped against the far shore of Walloha. Cleo stepped out and dragged it inland, where it would be ready to take her back to her tribe. She never considered that she might not be making a return trip across the lake.

"Okay, Cleo." She prepped herself. "Don't lose your cool. Just stay calm and talk reason."

Through a thicket of dry shrubs, Cleo saw several fires. The rhythmic pounding of drums wove through the hypnotic waves of Walloha licking at the shore beneath her feet. If Alex were watching, he'd be screaming at her right now to go back. She didn't hear his voice. She was alone. Cleo took a deep breath and bravely stepped forward.

"Who's this?" a voice said from the darkness. "Nez Perce scum trying to save herself?"

Before Cleo could respond, she was grabbed by a second Blackfoot warrior and pushed to her knees. The first Blackfoot knelt before Cleo, grabbed her hair, and bent her head back. His hate-filled black eyes burned into her own and his firm grip prevented Cleo from looking away.

"Want to be a slave?" he growled.

"Take me to Bloody Chief," Cleo demanded, mustering all her courage.

The two Blackfoot looked at each other, both surprised at Cleo's confidence and her demand. There was a moment of tense silence; then both warriors laughed. Cleo knew it was not a laugh of good humor. It was of cruelty.

Cleo was thrown to her knees once more. Rocks dug into her palms, and her hands stung as blood ran from the fresh scrapes. She was tired of being treated like a rag doll by the two Blackfoot warriors. They had dragged Cleo back to their camp. Her body ached and she wanted to fight back, but she knew her resistance had to come from determination, not anger.

"What's this dirt?" a voice said from above her.

Cleo looked up. Bloody Chief stood over her, with the same look of hatred the two warriors had given her. Cleo could feel the heat of the huge bonfire against her skin. She was now in the center of the Blackfoot encampment. Bloody Chief, in full ceremonial garb, was celebrating the day's victory and anticipating tomorrow's finality. He was surrounded by the tribe's elders and its greatest warriors, but right now, the young girl on her hands and knees was given the benefit of his full attention.

"I'm Seeloo," Cleo began.

"What are you doing here?" Bloody Chief demanded, then without waiting for her reply added, "Get her out of here."

The two warriors grabbed Cleo by the arms and roughly dragged her toward the darkness beyond the bonfire.

"I'm Red Wolf's daughter," Cleo called out.

The words caught Bloody Chief's attention. He raised a hand and his two warriors halted in their tracks.

"You're the daughter of a worm," Bloody Chief growled. "Why did the worm send you here?"

"He didn't."

"You think I'd save your hide?" Bloody Chief smiled.

"That's not why I came," Cleo told him, and pulled away from the two warriors who still held her arms.

"Then you'd better tell me why you did!" Bloody Chief was growing impatient.

Cleo took a moment and looked upon the faces of the elders and warriors surrounding her. Each one looked upon her as if she were less than human, a mere dung beetle they had found under a shoe and loathsomely scraped off on a nearby rock. Cleo's eyes locked on Bloody Chief.

"I hear your warriors singing and drumming, Bloody Chief. Imagine your village left silent," she began. "There are so few of us left. The spirits here, they'd be alone without their people. They'd listen, but there'd be nothing. And then, with no one to remember them, they too would fade away like the Nez Perce."

Tlesca stood to his father's right, staring at Cleo, never blinking, never turning away. His gaze wasn't filled with anger and hate like the others'. It was painted with understanding and admiration. He looked upon Cleo like a young man feeling the first aching hunger of love.

Cleo was unaware of her silent admirer and continued with her plea. "Where's the honor in killing old men and women and children? If you attack tomorrow, that's all you'll find."

Cleo and Bloody Chief stared at each other in a momentary silence that seemed to stretch into eternity. The long moments ate at her heart, and Cleo felt her spirit begin to die with the ebbing fire that had once burned so brightly in the camp's center.

He has to make peace, Cleo assured herself. *He has to.*

Bloody Chief stood. He looked down on Cleo. "Kill her quickly. That much mercy I will show."

The two warriors clenched Cleo by the head and shoulders, and they pushed her to her knees once again. While one warrior produced a large stone battle-ax, the second forced Cleo's head to the cold ground.

"Alex," she whispered, praying her brother could create some miracle to save her. But Alex was searching for Max Asher and was ignorant of his sister's plight. Cleo clenched her eyes shut.

She was afraid. And she was sad, too. Not for her own apparent demise, but that it would come before she would be able to find her father. She summoned a picture of him in her mind and focused on his face to calm herself.

The warrior raised the stone battle-ax above his head.

Chapter Seven

"No!" a voice shouted.

Cleo looked up and saw Tlesca race toward her. He skidded to his knees between Cleo and the ax blade and threw his robe over her shoulders—as if its animal hide and fur would somehow stand as a shield against the bladed weapon. This act of protection was not physical but symbolic. By throwing his robe across Cleo, the son of Bloody Chief had proclaimed himself her protector. Much to the dismay of his father.

"Tlesca!" Bloody Chief roared.

Father and son exchanged looks, then Bloody Chief stormed off to the edge of the encampment. Tlesca gave a wary look to his fellow Blackfoot, then followed his father.

"What was that about?" Bloody Chief demanded once Tlesca caught up to him.

"What was I supposed to do? Talk about it after she was dead?" Tlesca countered. "She came out of love for her people. She was prepared to die for them."

"You're too soft!" Bloody Chief could barely contain his rage at his son's words. "She's Red Wolf's daughter!"

"You hate him. I don't." Tlesca waited for a response, but Bloody Chief had none. The old warrior had never heard his son speak so about his old enemy, and now he was curious to see where this would lead. "As much as we hounded him out of buffalo country, as much as he was sick and starving, when it came time to fight, he didn't run. I faced him. I thought he'd be easy for me . . ."

Tlesca rubbed his shoulder and Bloody Chief eyed his bruise.

"That war club of his . . . ," Tlesca continued. "Shoulder'll never be right. . . ."

Bloody Chief stood like a marble statue, his features cold and unmoving.

"I can't hate a man for showing that kind of courage," Tlesca finished.

Cleo could hear the restrained voices of the father and son. She heard the tone from both sides, sometimes angry, other times persuading, but in the end she had no idea what fate awaited her. She dared not raise her head, afraid even the slightest show of resistance might somehow tip the scales against her. And when Bloody Chief once again stood over her, she continued to stare at the dirt.

The tiny dirt grains somehow became large, given enormous meaning because they might be the last things Cleo would ever see. Dirt. That was all she had to comfort her. Dirt and the memory of her loving father.

Cleo felt Bloody Chief's strong, calloused hands grab her hair. Her neck jerked back with such force, she feared that he intended to snap it himself. Bloody Chief stared into her eyes, never blinking, only searching. Cleo met his gaze with her own resolve, determined to show no weakness.

Finally, after a stretch of endless seconds, Cleo could feel the fist in her hair loosen its grip. Bloody Chief rose to his feet and, almost reluctantly, turned to his warriors.

"I see what my son sees," he pronounced, and laid his own beautiful fur robe over Cleo's shoulders. "Go home now and show your father my robe. He'll know what it means."

Cleo's heart stopped. *Was I that close?* she wondered. *I . . . almost died.* Her muscles, tight as guitar strings, went lax and she nearly fell to her knees with relief.

Cleo gave a silent nod and quickly left the Blackfoot camp. She had not been jogging back to the lake for more than a few minutes when she heard "Seeloo!" called out from behind her.

Someone ran after her. She saw a head bobbing and weaving through the tall grass, though in the dim moonlight, Cleo was uncertain who her pursuer was.

"I'm glad I caught you." It was Tlesca.

"Caught me?" Cleo asked.

"I wanted to see you again," he confessed.

"You did?"

Tlesca smiled and looked out across Walloha. The waters were flat and calm, as the lake usually was. The moon hung in the sky, a silvery guardian of the night. It threw its light onto the two youths, creating a soft glow on their skin and hair.

"You're very . . . beautiful," he finally added, looking back at Cleo. "But you must know that."

"Guess it's in the eye of the beholder," Cleo bashfully replied.

"I never heard it put that way."

"I have to go. My father—"

Tlesca cut Cleo off and grabbed her arm. "Not yet."

"Do I have a choice?" Cleo looked down at Tlesca's arm and wondered what she was in for now.

Tlesca followed her gaze and realized what he had done. "Yes. Sorry . . ." He released his grip and stared into Cleo's eyes, which made her more uncomfortable than his pressuring squeeze.

"What're you looking at?" she finally asked, unable to bear the silence.

"Tell me where you found it?" he questioned, still not looking away from her face.

"Found what?"

"The courage to face my father."

Cleo felt safe with Tlesca. He had, after all, saved her life at the possible risk of his own, but now was not the time for small talk. She had to get back to her own village before she was missed and the worst was assumed.

The last thing I need, Cleo thought as Tlesca dreamily stared at her, *is to put my butt on the line, then have the Nez Perce attack, thinking I've been kidnapped!*

"I really have to get back," she insisted.

"One more question," Tlesca called out as Cleo ran toward the lake. She stopped and he continued. "Have you given your heart to anyone?"

"You mean a guy?" Cleo wasn't sure who else there was to give your heart to and quickly realized how stupid the question sounded. "No . . . there is no guy. I came to your father to ask for peace. If he saw us together, it'd ruin everything."

"Might help." Tlesca considered the prospect and smiled. "When you hear this mourning dove on your shore, it'll be me."

He cupped his hands to his mouth and made a birdcall—or what was supposed to be a birdcall. It sounded more like a strong wind blowing through rusty blinds hung over a broken window.

"That was a mourning dove?" Cleo asked, not sure if that was the actual call or just a warm-up. "Sounded more mourning than dove."

"Not the greatest mourning dove call in the world, I know."

The two exchanged smiles, their different backgrounds brought a little closer by the small joke. Cleo gave Tlesca a reassuring nod and disappeared into the darkness, leaving the young chief-to-be alone with his thoughts and hopes.

Chapter Eight

Alex raced up the stairs two at a time. Max
Asher still wasn't answering his phone, and Alex
felt his best bet to track down the professor was
to search the university himself. Alex skidded
around the corner of the third-story flight and
bounded up the fourth without a second
thought. He burst from the stairwell into the
hallway and directly into Barbara Frazier.

"Well, hello," she said with surprise.

Alex had always gotten along with Barbara
before his dad disappeared, though he'd never

liked her much. But since Alex's dad had vanished, Barbara insisted that Matt Bellows had stolen something from the university and fled. Alex hadn't been able to look at Barbara again after her first insinuations.

"Hi, Barbara."

"Looking for me?"

"No," Alex responded. He couldn't believe he had ever liked this woman. Now, even her tone set him on edge.

"I'm here to see Max Asher. Do you know where he is?" Alex asked.

"What do you want with Max?" Now Barbara was really interested. Max was a friend of Alex's father and not just a colleague like Barbara had been. Obviously cogs in her head were turning with the possible meanings of Alex's query.

"I really gotta go."

"I was just curious," Barbara cut in, not allowing Alex to leave. "You look like you've just run a four-minute mile. I thought there might've been some kind of emergency."

"No. Everything's fine." Alex wondered if his resentment was as obvious as Barbara's suspicion.

"Max is at MIT until Friday. Guest lecturer. Anything I can do to help?"

The last person on earth Alex wanted help from was Barbara, but he realized at that point, she just might be the last person on earth who could help him.

"You know anything about Nez Perce Indians?"

"Yes." Her answer was quick and confident. "As it happens, it's an area I've focused on."

"I have an essay due tomorrow," Alex lied. He knew Barbara would inquire into his sudden interest and felt it best to head the question off early.

"And you're in a big hurry to get it done. I know," Barbara added, changing her tone to friendly. "Just make sure you tell your mother how helpful I'm being. I don't want to get another tongue-lashing for talking to you. So . . . ask away."

"I need stuff on the Nez Perce—Blackfoot wars," Alex hurriedly confessed. "Especially something on Red Wolf, Bloody Chief . . . Seeloo."

"Who?"

"Seeloo."

"You writing an essay on something make-believe?" Barbara asked, laughing.

"It's for Cultural Studies," Alex assured her.

"I've lectured on the Plains Indians' history extensively, Alex." Barbara's manner was that of a smug teacher speaking down to a rebellious student. "Bloody Chief, Red Wolf, Seeloo . . . I've never heard of them."

"Doesn't mean they didn't exist," Alex said sharply.

"Yes, it does," Barbara answered, sure of her intellectual superiority.

"Actually," Alex began, preparing to turn the tables on Barbara and trying his best not to allow a smile to escape, "Red Wolf was one of the Nez Perce's greatest chiefs and warriors. His daughter, Seeloo . . . well, she was a key factor in making peace with the Blackfoot."

"I don't know what you're talking about." Barbara's slight hesitation revealed cracks in her arrogant veneer.

"Maybe it's new stuff that's come to light in archaeological circles, Barbara. I don't know. I guess maybe we should both talk to Max about it. Anyway, I gotta go."

And with that, Alex raced back down the stairs and finally let himself enjoy the pleasure of a smile.

Chapter Nine

"**You have destroyed** my honor!" Red Wolf yelled.

That wasn't the response Cleo had been expecting. "Great!" maybe, or at least "thanks." But not this.

"Bloody Chief wants us defenseless. I don't trust him," Strong Bear said.

Cleo knew his words weighed heavily with Red Wolf and she acted quickly to sway the elders in her favor, in peace's favor.

"His son can be trusted," she informed them. "And Bloody Chief listens to him."

"He's just a boy," Red Wolf huffed. "And the son of my enemy!"

"What about Walloha?" Cleo reminded them. "Do you trust her? She told me to go. Or is the spirit of the lake your enemy, too?"

Red Wolf and Strong Bear paused. They exchanged a look and Red Wolf shook his head. Cleo could tell her last statement had struck a chord. Red Wolf had not softened, but perhaps there was hope.

"Why do the spirits come now?" Strong Bear growled. "Where were they when we prayed for their aid two moons ago? Or today?"

"What did Walloha say?" Red Wolf asked.

"And how do you know it was Walloha?" Strong Bear cut in, not allowing Cleo to answer. "Spirits are tricky. It might have even been a Blackfoot spirit!"

"She said she wanted to stop the fighting between the Blackfoot and the Nez Perce. She said peace was the only way for our people to survive." Cleo decided to skip the part about the sacrifice.

"Victory is the only way!" Strong Bear reminded everyone.

"I need to think," Red Wolf finally said, and exited the tipi.

"He'll think right," Strong Bear was quick to point out. "He hates Blackfoot."

"Is hate all you know?" Cleo shouted, and stormed from the tipi.

Cleo left Strong Bear and wandered through the small village. If Bloody Chief attacked tomorrow, there would be no hope for anyone. Peace was their only chance, and she prayed Red Wolf could realize that truth.

Cleo's meditations were broken by the sound of a mourning dove—a mourning dove in severe pain. It was Tlesca's signal. She headed down to Walloha and found him on the shore.

Tlesca rose from a thicket of bushes like a suitor hiding from his girlfriend's father. Cleo made sure no one had followed her, and she crunched into the thicket to meet Tlesca.

"What are you doing here?" she whispered.

"I couldn't sleep," Tlesca said, and motioned to a lone canoe beached on the shore. He took Cleo's hand in his own and led her to the water's edge.

"Go for a ride?" he asked.

Cleo nodded and Tlesca helped her into the canoe.

"Big day tomorrow," Cleo commented.

Tlesca pushed off from shore and quietly paddled to the lake's center.

"Why do you hate the Nez Perce?" Cleo asked.

Tlesca was shocked at the bluntness of the question, but was once again enamored by Cleo's boldness.

"I hate them because I was told to hate them. My father hates them, his father hated them, and his father's father did, too."

"And that makes sense to you?"

Tlesca thought for a moment. "It did. Why shouldn't it? Nez Perce people killed my friends, my relatives. Why shouldn't I believe them to be the monsters I am told they are?" Tlesca stopped paddling for a moment and looked at Cleo. "But then I met you. I heard your words, saw what you did, and I realized that a heart of such love and courage could never beat within the body of a monster."

"All that in one day?" Cleo was surprised by the suddenness of the transformation.

"Should it take more than a moment for a man to realize he was wrong? Should it take more than a day for a man to want change?" Tlesca spoke wisely. "Our people still hate. They are still blind. Only you and I can see the truth, Seeloo. We must show them the way."

"I will, Tlesca," Cleo assured him. "Are you nervous about tomorrow? Is that why you came?"

"It's not because of that. I had to talk to you," he confessed. "I've never been so sure of anything in my life."

Cleo took a moment to admire Tlesca. In his face, she saw strength and determination, but it was tempered by kindness. He was an amazing person, not just because he had saved her life, but because he was choosing life over death and war.

"What are you so sure of?" Cleo finally asked.

"My father's a hard man, but I'll get through to him." Cleo felt Tlesca was talking more to himself than to her, trying to convince himself that the path he had chosen was a walkable one. He stared off toward the distant shore.

"Get what through to him?" Cleo asked. "I'm sorry, Tlesca, I don't understand what—"

"I want to take you to my lodge, Seeloo," Tlesca said, breaking his gaze away from the horizon and returning his eyes to Cleo.

"I don't think going to your lodge right now would be too smart. Not after what happened."

Tlesca nodded. The paddle sliced into the water in a repeated rhythm that lulled Cleo into a drifting feeling of sanctuary.

"I don't have my own lodge. Not yet," Tlesca added, and smiled at Cleo.

The words and smile sank deeper than Tlesca's other musings and suddenly Cleo realized there was much more going on here than she had assumed.

"Tlesca," she began. "Are you asking me to marry you?"

Chapter Ten

"Shhh!" the librarian hissed at Alex.

"Sorry," Alex sheepishly said as he picked up several dropped books from the floor.

Alex had left the university and headed straight for the library. Shelf after shelf stood before him with thousands upon thousands of books, but all he needed was the one that would tell him what happened to Seeloo.

Alex found five that might help, and he raced back home to digest their contents and check on Cleo. He burst through the front door and nearly ran over his mother, Lily, coming out.

"What's the hurry, Alex?" she asked.

"Gotta study," Alex replied, and waved the books before her to offer undeniable proof of his claim.

"Well, take a break and help me unload groceries from the car."

"Mom! I can't! I'm in panic mode. Big essay due!"

"Five minutes, and you can blame any bad grade on me."

Alex hesitated, handed his books to his mother, and raced back out the door. Lily juggled the stack for a moment, then peered down at the cover of the one on top.

"Nez Perce?" she asked Alex as he trudged back into the house under the weight of several bags of food.

"Yeah. Real interesting stuff," Alex huffed, and unloaded his burden on the kitchen table.

Lily followed him into the kitchen and handed back his stack of books. "I played that part at camp."

Alex froze in his tracks. "What part?"

"We used to do these little plays the

counselors wrote," Lily continued, ignoring Alex's direct question.

Lily called up a Nez Perce dance from her memory and did a quick three-feet-between-us, straight-arm ritual. She stopped after a few movements and laughed.

"Or something like that . . ." She trailed off.

"Okay, Mom, what happened?" Alex asked.

"We sat together the whole time on the hayride." A wave of nostalgia crashed upon Lily's face. "He tried to kiss me, but I hit him."

"I mean the play?" Alex stressed, doing his best to extend his patience well beyond its normal boundaries. "What happened in the play?"

"It was beautiful." Lily smiled wistfully. "Seeloo is this Native American girl who falls in love with a boy from the other side of the tracks. Or I guess the other side of the lake, to be more exact."

Lily smiled at her own joke. Alex offered a courtesy smile, then urged his mother to continue.

"It's kinda like *Romeo and Juliet*," Lily said.

"How so?"

"Well, two fighting families, lots of hatred, but in the center of it all, these two kids find love. And in the end, the two tribes, the Blackfoot and the Nez Perce, find peace."

"That's it?" Alex asked, relieved that his worst fears might not be realized. "That's not so bad."

"What do you mean 'that's it'? It's a beautiful story," Lily informed him. "Seeloo sacrifices her life for peace."

Alex dropped the books. They slammed against the kitchen floor with a resounding clap. He stepped toward Lily with a frightful urgency, unsure how even to ask the question he had to ask.

"How, Mom? How does Seeloo die?"

"Why, Alex . . . ," Lily started, taken aback by her son's sudden intensity. "Seeloo drowns."

Chapter Eleven

The canoe floated on the lake like a cloud. The cool waters of Walloha caressed Cleo's hand, gently bidding her to dip it deeper. Cleo wondered if she was dreaming. The problems of her handicap were a distant memory, and even the horrors of yesterday's battle were fading like a gentle mist before the morning sun.

"Yes," she reasoned aloud. "I must be dreaming."

"I want us to be together, Seeloo." It was Tlesca. His words pulled Cleo from her momentary reverie. She became more aware of her surroundings, and Lake Walloha's urging was silenced.

"You're very handsome, but—"

"In the eye of the beholder," Tlesca reminded her.

"But—"

"What do you fear?" Tlesca would not back down. He gently touched Cleo's wrist. "Us being found out and losing the peace? We will be the ones who make the peace hold!"

Tlesca seemed earnest in his desires for Seeloo and peace. He truly believed this was their fathers' war, not theirs, and he had no intention of inheriting his father's hatred. He gently stroked Cleo's hair, using his touch to assure her that their union would indeed bring peace.

"How old are you, Tlesca?"

"Eighteen. You?"

"Fifteen." Cleo's voice sharpened on the word. She was supposed to be thinking about weekend plans with friends, not marriages to Indian princes.

"I'm sorry you had to wait this long," Tlesca replied. His words shocked Cleo, but then she remembered this was a different time, a different culture. Fifteen wasn't too young to be married, it was almost too old! "If only we had met sooner," Tlesca lamented.

"Wow." The word was more breath than speech.

" 'Wow?' Does that mean 'yes' in your language?" Tlesca was searching for any clue to Cleo's feelings for him.

"Sometimes."

Cleo was unsure. This wasn't her life; it was Seeloo's. Cleo intended to make things right in Seeloo's world and end the war, not desert her to some marriage she never intended to join. In her heart, Cleo felt Tlesca would be a good husband, a man of nobility and fairness, but the decision to marry him should fall to Seeloo, not Cleo.

Tlesca looked at Cleo with expecting eyes. She was about to ask for time to think when Alex's voice thundered in her head.

"Get off the water, Cleo! Now!"

Cleo covered her mouth and chastised her brother with a harsh whisper. "Quiet!"

"You gotta listen to me," Alex pressed. "Seeloo drowns!"

Cleo's face drained to an ashen white. She snatched her hand back from the water as if a sharp-toothed fish had suddenly risen from the deep and bitten a finger.

"What?" Tlesca asked, aware of her sudden change in mood.

"I gotta get back."

They weren't exactly the words Tlesca wanted to hear, but he understood. The war between their people was more important than both of them, and for now their needs had to be placed second.

Tlesca paddled the canoe to the shore and helped Cleo onto dry land.

"I'll be back in the morning," he assured her, then made the trek back across Lake Walloha.

"Did you hear what I said?" Alex asked urgently the moment Tlesca disappeared in the darkness.

"Yeah." Cleo sighed. "Who told you that?"

"It's a long story, but it's true. It's what happens. We need to get you out of there. Do you remember the artifact you touched on the plasma screen when you first went in?"

"No." Cleo's voice was heavy with concern.

"Think, Cleo!"

"I am thinking, Alex! I don't know! I just wheeled over to the screen and touched it."

"That's not good enough, Cleo."

"What am I supposed to do?" Cleo yelled back. "Just wander around the village touching everything I see until I get it right?"

"Well, what else are you going to do? You shouldn't even be there! You should've listened to me and not—"

"Alex . . ." Cleo cut him off, her voice softened by a growing fear. She asked the question neither sibling really wanted to answer. "If Seeloo drowns . . . what happens to me?"

Chapter Twelve

The sun rose on the Nez Perce village. It was a new day, but the warmth of the sun's rays flooding through the trees and over the hill could not wash away the pain and suffering that had befallen the Nez Perce only one day earlier.

The dead had been buried, the wounded tended; some lay floating between life and death, unwilling to let go of this world, certain that their purpose here had yet to be fulfilled.

Cleo awoke at dawn. The air was still cool and dew clung to the grass outside her tipi. She greeted the first glimmer of sunlight and immediately saw Red Wolf, Strong Bear, and a handful of the remaining warriors capable of fighting. They gathered in the center of the village, armed for battle.

"Red Wolf!" Cleo yelled, and raced up. Red Wolf threw her a strange look and Cleo quickly realized her error. "Father . . . ," she corrected. "Father. You prepare to fight before you have even heard Bloody Chief's words of peace."

"No, daughter. I prepare for betrayal." Red Wolf turned to his warriors. "But none of you shall raise your weapons until I *do* hear Bloody Chief's words." Red Wolf inhaled and tasted the sweet, pure air. He looked to the cloudless sky and let the wind play with the long strands of his silver hair. "It is a good day to die," he added. "But it is an even better day to make peace."

Cleo smiled.

The group headed down to Lake Walloha, where the canoes of Bloody Chief, Tlesca, and the Blackfoot warriors were nearly ashore.

"Be ready," Strong Bear warned the Nez Perce warriors. "We don't trust the Blackfoot!"

"Quiet, Strong Bear," Red Wolf admonished under his breath.

Bloody Chief and his warriors dragged their canoes ashore. They outnumbered Red Wolf's men two to one. If they had come for a fight, it would be short and brutal. Men on both sides would die, and without a miracle, it would be the last day Red Wolf walked the earth.

"Why are your men armed?" Bloody Chief demanded. "You've seen our tokens of peace."

Before the negotiations had even started, Bloody Chief was already angry. Cleo was about to step forward and offer reassurance, but Red Wolf spoke.

"You have weapons."

"We've won!" Bloody Chief explained. "We have the right to be armed and you do not. We could kill all of you if we chose."

Cleo knew his words were true. She prayed that Bloody Chief would not have to prove they could be much more than a threat.

"You returned my daughter to me last night . . . ," Red Wolf said. His words were slow. He was trying to convince himself that what he was about to do was the right choice, the best choice.

Cleo's eyes widened in amazement as Red Wolf slowly lowered his famous war club, the weapon he had carried with him for so many moons. It was like an extension of Red Wolf's arm. He turned the handle toward Bloody Chief and silently offered it to the victorious leader.

Bloody Chief stared at the club for a moment, then carefully pushed it aside.

"Seeloo has warrior blood like her father," Bloody Chief explained. "I won't take your club, Red Wolf. If I'm going to make peace with my enemy, I want him strong."

Red Wolf nodded. "Then we shall talk."

A dam burst inside Cleo and a crashing wave of relief flooded through her body. She felt her legs grow rubbery as the tension raced from her limbs.

She caught Tlesca's eye. And the two exchanged small smiles of hope.

Red Wolf led the way back to his lodge, Bloody Chief at his side. The trust was not strong between the two groups, but if it was enough to hold through a truce, all would be well.

Cleo's smile grew larger.

"It's not going to happen, Seeloo," a bitter voice sounded behind her. She spun and faced Strong Bear. "No matter what spirit you talked to."

Strong Bear sneered at Cleo, then slowly made his way after the others, leaving a leaden feeling of despair in his wake.

Chapter Thirteen

The two groups of warriors crowded into Red Wolf's lodge. Although they sat close, like brothers, the air was thick with tension and seething anger. Red Wolf and Bloody Chief sat in the center. They were each flanked by their elders and warriors. Tlesca sat to his father's right and Cleo did her best to stay out of the way.

She wanted to help, wanted to sit between both sides and hammer out an agreement, but she knew that was not her place in this culture. She was expected to bring the men food and drink, and she did, but she was ready to aid Tlesca should the need arise. She hoped it would not.

Cleo hated being silent. She knew Tlesca could work out an agreement between the two tribes, but the resentment ran so deep, Tlesca would need all the help he could get. Cleo touched his shoulder to signal her support. He gripped her hand with his own. Cleo handed him a drink and he returned a smile.

"When I was a boy, my grandfather told me about the battle at Two Rivers Crossing," Tlesca began. His voice was light, but it showed respect for the memory and for Red Wolf, to whom he was speaking. "We were the ones outnumbered then."

"My father was there," Red Wolf coolly informed the young man.

Where Tlesca was eager and open, Red Wolf's attitude was closer to the others in the tipi. He could not afford to show a crack, an opening of weakness his adversaries could use against him.

"My grandfather walked with a limp after that battle." Tlesca grinned, but he was alone in his efforts to ease the hostility. "We tell stories about your father, Red Wolf."

Red Wolf raised his mighty war club. "This was once his."

"Yes," Tlesca commented, and rubbed his sore shoulder, which had unfortunately been on the receiving end of the wolf-headed club. "It's famous in our family."

Red Wolf's cold face did not change with Tlesca's kind words of admiration. The old warrior turned to Bloody Chief as if to say "Let us begin."

"Two Rivers Crossing was long ago," Bloody Chief said. "Today, you are the ones outnumbered. What do I gain by making peace with you? We won't leave here empty-handed."

The negotiations began and Cleo moved next to Red Wolf. She sat quietly at his side, hoping she would not be dismissed. She knew the Indian warriors did not consider a meeting of warriors a place for a girl, but she hoped her status as the chief's daughter would afford her some flexibility—and perhaps even allow participation.

"The Nez Perce can't live on fish alone. We need meat," Red Wolf was quick to point out.

"Maybe we could let you fish here if you let us hunt buffalo," Cleo meekly offered, hoping to help push the détente forward.

"Buffalo country is Blackfoot country." Bloody Chief was mildly surprised anyone would be so bold as to suggest they share this precious resource.

"Not when I was a boy." Red Wolf glared.

"You are no longer a boy, Red Wolf." Bloody Chief's words were firm. "You started all this, ambushing Blackfoot people at their campsites . . ."

Strong Bear broke his silence. "My father told a different story! We were the ones picked off!"

"We're trying to move beyond—"

Tlesca cut off Cleo's words. "This war has cost our tribes too much. Losses on both sides." He jumped in and tried to calm the waters, but Strong Bear was determined to continue.

"Not enough losses on your side . . . ," he grumbled.

Red Wolf placed a hand on Strong Bear's shoulder, silencing his volatile warrior. "Life is not worth living if we don't hunt buffalo," Red Wolf calmly explained.

"We shall camp at this lake whenever we want. You can hunt buffalo on our lands, but not when we're there." Bloody Chief crossed his arms to emphasize the finality of his offer.

"When you're not there? You're always there," Red Wolf objected. "And Lake Walloha has been with our people . . . always."

"Details can be settled later," Tlesca cut in, realizing things were not going in the direction he wanted. "What's important now is that there be an agreement to make peace."

Red Wolf boiled. He gripped the war club in his hands and fought his growing desire to throw the lot of Blackfoot from his lodge and his land.

"There can be no such agreement without the will on your father's part to compromise," Red Wolf warned.

"He's making an offer, we can work with that," Cleo urged.

Bloody Chief turned to his son. A fierceness crept across his face. "The only reason I'm sitting in his lodge is that you took it upon yourself to save her life!" Bloody Chief's rage grew as the words passed his lips.

"With no regrets, Father! None!" Tlesca shouted back.

Bloody Chief erupted from his sitting place. "No more talk," he growled, and stormed from the tipi.

Like water gushing from an uncorked bottle,

the rest of the Blackfoot warriors flowed out behind Bloody Chief. Tlesca followed suit, casting a heavy look back at Cleo.

"Father, there must be more we can do," Cleo coaxed.

"More?" Red Wolf answered. "He can kill us quickly today, or kill us slowly with his offer. Either way, he only seeks to end our people."

"If he had intended that, they would have come in war, not peace. We can work with them—"

Red Wolf would hear no more. He raised his hand to silence Cleo. She saw his hand grow red as his grip tightened on his war club. Red Wolf left the tipi and his warriors followed suit. At the mouth of the tipi, Strong Bear stopped for a moment and looked back at Cleo.

An "I told you so" grin sliced across his determined face, then he ducked under the tipi opening and followed his chief.

Chapter Fourteen

"We were close!" Tlesca said to Bloody Chief, who strode before him like a noble lion marching back to its lair.

Bloody Chief stopped in his tracks and turned toward Tlesca. "Before this madness, we were close to having everything we've fought for anyway! We are the victors, yet now we sit with words and ask for what is rightfully ours from battle."

Bloody Chief spun around once more and marched toward his canoe. Red Wolf and his warriors watched the Blackfoot leave, still wary of their intentions.

"He wants no part of peace," Strong Bear warned.

"Talk to Bloody Chief," Cleo urged, racing up to Red Wolf. "Just you and him." She threw a look at Strong Bear. She knew he was poison in Red Wolf's ear. "You don't need me there, or Tlesca." She glared at Strong Bear and added, "Or anyone else. The two of you can figure this out, Father!"

Red Wolf didn't hesitate. He turned to Strong Bear and said, "Tell the men to be ready."

"But Father, I—"

Red Wolf would hear no more. Cleo's meddling had nearly cost her life, and certainly some of Red Wolf's pride. He unleashed an angry glare on Cleo and silenced her.

"You stay here," he warned.

And with that, Red Wolf left.

Cleo felt helpless. She kicked the dirt and plopped on the ground. "Now what?" She huffed. She was used to history exams and high school, not stopping a bloody war between two angry tribes. The rage on both sides ran deep and was certainly more powerful than the desire to use words instead of weapons to solve this problem. Cleo understood this, but she searched her mind for some new strategy she could try.

"Cleo." She heard a whisper in her head.

"Walloha?" she whispered back.

"Just me." It was Alex.

"What are we going to do?" she asked.

"Get you out of there, that's what."

"I can't go! I can't desert them!"

"This isn't your fight, Cleo."

"I don't want it to be a fight," she corrected her brother. "I want it to be peace!"

"I may have a way to get you out of there," he said, not wanting to debate the issue.

Back in their father's study, Alex printed out several pages on a LaserWriter. He could see Cleo on the plasma screen, see her look of growing frustration.

"Dad kept text files of everything in the CyberMuseum. I'm printing out the Plains Indians room. Northern tribes."

"What for?" Cleo asked.

"To help you remember what you touched. Now listen." Alex pulled the pages from the LaserWriter. The list of items was long, but one of them had to be the artifact Cleo had touched. Alex read the alphabetized list. "Buffalo robe, buffalo-bone spearhead . . ."

Cleo's thoughts drifted. She heard Alex move through the alphabet, but the words floated through her head and out her ear. Her focus was someplace else, and getting out of the myth and back to her world just didn't seem that important to her. Setting things right mattered now.

"Alex . . ."

"Eagle headdress, fire bow drill . . ." Alex ignored her and stuck to the list.

"I can't come home yet," Cleo told him. She stood and headed for the lake. "There's more I have to do here."

Alex heard her but hoped that if he could just find the object she had touched, she'd forget about doing anything and come home. He doubled his reading pace.

"Animal-tooth saw or weapon, stone-grinding tool, stone statue . . ."

"I told you I don't remember, Alex! Stop reading!"

"Think, Cleo! Think!" he yelled, upset that his sister wasn't cooperating with his efforts to bring her back. "Think about Mom. Two missing persons in one family? She'll lose it. Completely."

Alex's words pierced Cleo like an arrow. She stopped and thought of her mother . . . and her father. How was any of this helping to find him? Had she gotten so caught up in the myth's drama, she had forgotten what was most important to her and her own family? Alex's seeds of doubt grew in her head.

"Okay," she conceded. "I'll try to help Tlesca *and* look for the artifact I touched. Don't worry, Alex. You won't be an only child anytime soon."

"After today, being an only child doesn't sound like such a bad idea," Alex joked.

Cleo headed after Red Wolf. He and his warriors had caught up to Bloody Chief and the Blackfoot just outside the village.

"Nothing until my signal," Bloody Chief warned his people when he saw his pursuers.

"Do not attack unless they attack," Red Wolf told his warriors as they approached the Blackfoot.

"Why do you follow us?" Bloody Chief asked.

"Why do you leave?" Red Wolf countered.

"We leave because you dance with your words. We are the victors. We should determine the spoils of war."

As the two men exchanged words, Cleo made her way around a small hill and spotted the groups. *At least they haven't started fighting yet,* she reassured herself.

She gave a deep sigh and was about to move closer when she heard a slight crack above her head. She looked up, and in a nearby tree was a Nez Perce warrior. His bow was drawn. His arm twitched from the tension on the string. An arrow was in place, and he stood at the ready like a watchful sentry.

Cleo immediately recognized the trouble. There was only one reason for a warrior to be hiding in a tree, arrow drawn: treachery. She raced toward the tree, not exactly sure what to do once she got there. Try to pull him down, perhaps? He was a Nez Perce warrior, so she knew he would never hurt the chief's daughter—or so she hoped.

Strong Bear saw Cleo speeding toward the tree and gave a small, quick hand signal. Cleo never saw Strong Bear, but she did see the warrior in the tree tense up and pull the bow back even harder. Cleo's legs felt like lead, unwilling to cooperate, and time slowed.

Cleo saw the warrior's fingers move. She saw the sun glint off the sharp black arrowhead. She heard herself scream "No!"—or thought it was she who screamed it. Who else would have? Who else knew what was about to happen, what Cleo was helpless to prevent?

The arrow bolted from the bow and sailed through the air with deadly purpose. Cleo crashed to the pine needles that covered the ground. She pounded her fist against the uncaring earth and was afraid to look up, to see the arrow's path, to watch it hit its target.

And hit its target it did.

Chapter Fifteen

The arrow sank into the back of a Blackfoot warrior. He fell, dead before he hit the dirt. Strong Bear's betrayal had succeeded. He did not want peace. He did not want talk. He had put the Nez Perce assassin in the tree to start a fight, and that was exactly what he got.

Before the unfortunate Blackfoot had even hit the ground, his fellow warriors had drawn their weapons and charged, hungry for vengeance. The Nez Perce warriors, despite the fact that most of them were shocked at the sneak attack by their own side, countered. The Indians released war cries and charged one another. Arms flailed, swinging axes and clubs with the wanton zeal of rage.

The fighting spread like fire through dry brush. Cleo watched Blackfoot stab Nez Perce and Nez Perce club Blackfoot. The scene was a horrible explosion of violence that vomited onto the land.

Cleo ran into the fight. She grabbed the arm of a Nez Perce warrior.

"No!" she shouted. "Stop fighting!"

The warrior shrugged her off like a fly. He swung his bone club over his head and smashed it into the side of a Blackfoot. The Blackfoot folded over and Cleo flinched at the cracking of his ribs.

"What are you doing?" Alex shouted. "They'll kill you! Get out of there!"

"I've got to stop this!" Cleo shouted back.

"How? By asking them?"

"If that's the only way . . . yes!" Cleo knew her words were insane, but she couldn't sit on the sidelines while people died. She didn't know if she was being brave or stupid; she just knew she had to help.

An arrow sizzled into the ground next to

Cleo. She jumped back and saw the Blackfoot warrior who had shot the arrow draw a second one from his quiver. This time he would not miss.

Cleo grabbed a small log from a burned-out fire and charged the Blackfoot. She let out a scream, not so much to scare him as to release the surging wave of fear that grew in her body.

The warrior loaded the arrow and pulled back the string. Cleo raised the log over her head. The warrior aimed. Cleo swung. The warrior's fingers released the string. Cleo's wild swing smashed the bow the instant the arrow began to move. Her follow-through hurled the log to the ground and she gasped for air, terrified that she had just looked death in the eye.

But her fight was not finished.

The warrior's bow was shattered, but his knife was not. He pulled it from his leather sheath and brandished the stone blade before Cleo.

"Run, Cleo!" Alex screamed.

"We don't have to do this . . . ," Cleo told the warrior, but he was in no mood to listen.

He slashed his blade at Cleo and she leapt back, barely escaping its cutting edge. Cleo swung her fist at the warrior, and he easily parried with his open hand. He turned the knife over and stabbed upward, slashing through the leather sleeve of Cleo's clothing.

Cleo gasped in shock and checked her arm. No blood. This time. The warrior sized her up and took a step forward. Cleo matched him by taking a step back. The warrior lunged, catching Cleo by surprise and tackling her. She kicked and punched, trying to get out from under her opponent, but he was too strong. He raised the knife and Cleo saw the dull, yellowing bone blade through panicked eyes.

The warrior fell to the side.

Cleo gasped for air as if she had just swum from the bottom of the ocean and broken the surface. The air surged in and filled her lungs with a sweet burning.

Strong Bear stood above her, brandishing his club.

"Seems my saving you is becoming a habit," he said.

"You wouldn't have to save anybody if you hadn't started this!" Cleo spat back.

"I started nothing, Seeloo. I merely sped up the inevitable. Do not blame me if you cannot see that."

Cleo raised her hand for Strong Bear to

help her up. He looked at her hand for a moment, then turned away.

"It would be wise of you to forget what you saw in the tree and leave the battlefield," he warned. "Next time, I may think twice before sparing your hide."

Strong Bear raced back into the fray, leaving Cleo to handle herself. She stood and quickly followed Strong Bear, but when he ran right to attack a Blackfoot, Cleo headed left to push a Nez Perce warrior off a wounded Blackfoot. The Nez Perce was shocked that the daughter of Red Wolf would help the enemy, but he would never raise a hand against the daughter of his chief. He cursed Cleo and bolted toward another Blackfoot. Cleo rolled the injured Blackfoot warrior onto his back, and he thanked her with a right hook to the jaw.

An exploding pain rocketed through Cleo's head. Alex had given up screaming at her long ago, and he watched helplessly as his sister crumpled to the ground. The Blackfoot warrior had no idea Cleo had intended to help him. Would he have cared? He saw the enemy and lashed out.

Cleo grabbed her aching chin. Her vision blurred and the warriors fighting around her suddenly looked like ghosts, fading in and out in a mystical dance of life and death. One of the ghosts charged toward Cleo. A pain echoed through her head and opened floodgates of confusion. The ghost dove next to Cleo. She was certain this was the end. She was too disoriented to fight back. Death seemed to be her only choice.

Chapter Sixteen

"Get behind me!" a voice cried.

Cleo's vision sharpened again as the hazy clouds left her brain. It was no ghost beside her. It was Tlesca. He had seen Cleo get hit and immediately raced to her side. He drew his club and protected Cleo with his body. The injured Blackfoot who had punched Cleo tried to stand. Tlesca kicked him to the ground.

"Get away from her!" he shouted.

A spear sailed through the air and stabbed the ground at Tlesca's feet.

"No!" Cleo cried out, fearing the next one would hit Tlesca.

Tlesca pulled the spear from the ground and waved it at a Nez Perce warrior, then spun and jabbed it toward one of his own Blackfoot allies, chasing both away. Tlesca was frantic, crazed, fending off anyone who would dare hurt Seeloo.

Bloody Chief heard his son cry out. He spun around, fearing the worst. Nothing could have prepared him for the sight that greeted his rage-filled eyes.

Tlesca stood alone, defending the daughter of Bloody Chief's hated enemy with his very life. Bloody Chief froze.

"What trick is this?" he growled. "Stop!" he shouted with such force, the trees themselves seemed to sway backward.

Red Wolf saw Bloody Chief calling off his warriors. With lightning reflexes, he grabbed the arm of a Nez Perce about to fire an arrow.

"Enough!" Red Wolf called out.

Bloody Chief lowered his weapon and stormed to Tlesca.

"What are you doing? What are you doing?" he shouted at his son.

"You'll kill me before you touch one hair on

her head!" Tlesca defiantly shouted back at his enraged father.

Silence cut through both tribes. Some Blackfoot and Nez Perce warriors even exchanged confused looks, hoping that someone, anyone, from either side could explain what was happening.

"I don't believe this . . ." Alex's words trailed off in Cleo's head.

"Believe it," she whispered back.

Tlesca rose before his father and stared into his eyes like a matador facing down a charging bull. But Bloody Chief was not charging, not anymore. He stood, swaying like a broken toy.

"I see . . ." was all he could say.

Red Wolf approached and lifted Cleo onto her feet. Like Bloody Chief's, his expression was one of dismay and confusion.

"Is it true?" he asked.

"He . . ." Cleo didn't know what to say, how to describe what seemed impossible. "He has feelings for me."

Red Wolf glared at Tlesca as any protective father might. Bloody Chief stepped forward, and for a moment, Cleo thought the two enemies would join forces to bring her and

Tlesca in line, teach the two teenagers who made the rules.

Tlesca stood his ground, facing both men, and Cleo stepped out from behind him to show her support of his courage. The four stood off until Red Wolf and Bloody Chief stopped being tribal leaders and became parents.

"She means that much to you, Tlesca?" Bloody Chief asked.

"Yes, Father."

"And you, Seeloo?" Red Wolf asked.

"I stand at his side."

Red Wolf leaned closer to Cleo. "No one will question the peace if you marry this boy, Seeloo," he asked. "Will you do that?"

"No!" It was Alex, not Cleo, but luckily no one could hear his protest except his sister. "Peace means sacrifice!"

All eyes turned to Cleo, and none with more anticipation than those of Red Wolf and Bloody Chief. The world around Cleo fell silent. This was much more than a commitment to marriage. It was an end to war. It was peace. It was the dawning of a new day. But it was also death— Seeloo's and possibly her own.

Thoughts raced through Cleo's mind. She

didn't know the myth—or whether Seeloo did love Tlesca—but now, if only this one time in this one instant, it was Cleo's choice. The results would be the same, wouldn't they? Marriage, peace, death. Cleo's heart pounded in her chest like a stampede of wild stallions.

Over Red Wolf's shoulder, Cleo suddenly recognized Walloha, the spirit of the lake. Cleo reached out to her with her eyes and Walloha answered with a soft smile that calmed Cleo's heart and salved her burning fears. Walloha nodded.

"Seeloo?" Red Wolf said, breaking the silence.

"Yes, Father. I will marry Tlesca."

"No!" Alex shouted, but his cry fell upon deaf ears.

Chapter Seventeen

The drums pounded against the darkness of the night. On the same ground where, mere days before, there had been screams of anguish and pain, there was now singing and joy. A bonfire leapt toward the stars, its flames licking at the sheltering sky, then sighing into oblivion.

Warriors laid down their axes and lifted drums. Nez Perce danced with Blackfoot. Enemies sang as one and their spirits lifted each of them beyond the dreadful memory of the war.

Cleo wore a beautiful deerskin dress, gracefully decorated with beads and feathers. She silently stood next to Tlesca, who wore his own ceremonial robe. Over the young couple arched a braided length of branches, held high over their heads by Blackfoot and Nez Perce warriors.

Cleo's stomach refused to stay still and did a continuous parade of backflips. Even though Cleo was walking in the moccasins of Seeloo, this still felt like her own wedding. She couldn't help feeling nervous, and she sensed even the brave Tlesca was jittery.

Tlesca had fought in numerous wars, but love could bring the greatest warrior to his knees and make him a gentle pup.

Two torchbearers stood on either side of Cleo and Tlesca. Cleo could feel the flame heat her skin. Her hand, clenched in Tlesca's, was generously coated in sweat—which Cleo was sure was met by Tlesca's own nervous contribution.

"Five days ago I buried my last son," an older woman moaned, startled by the twist fate had dealt. "And now we make peace with them?"

Another woman scratched her head and shrugged. They were not the only ones confused by this sudden turn of events.

The thunder of pounding drums and the

voices of song that accompanied Cleo and Tlesca as they moved before Red Wolf and Bloody Chief cut short the women's confusion.

The ritual was short and both chiefs enacted the rites of their tribes. Red Wolf, resplendent in the full ceremonial headdress signifying his status as chief, held out a bouquet of dried sage and sweet grass. One of the torchbearers met the offering with his torch, and the ends began to glow with the life of flame. Bloody Chief took the smoldering herbs and waved them over the heads of Cleo and Tlesca, creating a symbolically protective circle of smoke. He muttered several passages in his native tongue and then offered a final blessing.

"Now you are one," he said, and dropped the burning plants to his side. "The blood of one flows into the other."

"Drink this." Red Wolf offered a clay wedding vase filled with liquid. "It is the sacred water of our life-giving Walloha."

Cleo took the vase from Red Wolf with shaking hands. She raised the vase, then stopped. From the corner of her eye, she caught Strong Bear glaring at her. *Is he up to something?* she wondered. *Will he try to stop this?*

But Cleo realized no one would fight against the children of the chiefs when both chiefs stood behind them. Strong Bear and his kind were alone now, with only their hatred to give them counsel.

Cleo moved the vase to her lips and drank deeply of the cool water inside.

"Great," she heard Alex comment. "My sister's a teenage bride."

Tlesca lifted the vase from his bride's hands and took a deep draft. He lowered the ceremonial vessel and drew Cleo forward into an enveloping hug.

Both tribes burst into joyful cheers for the newlyweds.

Cleo looked into the stern face of Bloody Chief, the face feared by friend and foe alike. Bloody Chief looked upon the young Cleo, and for a moment, she thought he was fighting a smile.

Her heart soared through the clouds. She had done it. She and Tlesca had melted the frozen hearts of two great warriors and shown them the true value of life.

"This is not good," Alex reminded her.

Cleo's mood crashed to the ground.

"You pay too big a price for this, Cleo," Alex continued. "What are you getting yourself into? There's no turning back now."

Alex's words cut, and in the wound grew a deeper realization of her actions. Tomorrow she was to climb into a canoe with Tlesca and . . . what? Paddle to his home to build a lodge? Start a new life with the Blackfoot? Be a wife to the future chief and mother to their children? Or fill her lungs with the chilled waters of Lake Walloha, drown in the murky depths that waited silently for her with the patience of a stalking lion.

Was she not, after all, the sacrifice?

Chapter Eighteen

The sun rose. It was a simple thing that happened every day of Cleo's life, yet today was the first day she truly appreciated the significance.

She stretched and felt her limbs protest the first movements of morning. She lifted her arms above her head and extended her fingers skyward.

"Good morning, sleepyhead," Alex chimed in.

"Mornin'," Cleo mumbled.

"Please tell me you're not getting in that canoe."

Cleo didn't reply. She dressed and checked her hair.

"Alex," she finally replied. "This is Seeloo's

story, too. I can't destroy that. We've made the peace. Aren't these many lives more important than the one?"

"Not when the one is my sister trapped in a crazy myth!"

Cleo ended the conversation and exited the tipi.

Tlesca and Red Wolf were preparing Seeloo's things for the journey. Bloody Chief was already lakeside.

The world seemed sharper to Cleo, with new meaning. She had never thought agreeing to Walloha's deal would make her feel like this, make her feel like she was living the first day of her life.

Sounds were crisper, the air sweeter, the sun warmer. *Why couldn't I appreciate these things like this before?* Cleo wondered.

"It's strange," she said, hoping Alex was still watching.

"What?" He was.

"Sometimes you really don't know how to live until it's time to die . . ." Cleo's words trailed off.

"Don't speak that way, Cleo," Alex chastised. "This is the last chance we might have to get you out of there. I'm going down the CyberMuseum's inventory again."

Alex reread the list and this time Cleo listened more intently. She gave one ear to Alex and joined her husband—she still wasn't used to the idea—and Red Wolf as they walked to Lake Walloha.

"I'll come visit before the thaw," Red Wolf assured her, doing his best to hide his sadness.

"Goodbye . . . Father," Cleo replied, her own words dripping with sorrow that this might be the closest she would ever come to speaking to her own father again.

And if this really were her own father, what would Cleo say to him? If this were the last time she saw him before he got lost in a myth, as she was now? What words would she say? How could she ever express what she felt for him?

"Please . . . ," she said to herself. "Please give me that chance."

Cleo looked at the waiting canoe. Bright colors and carved wood made it a vessel worthy of carrying the children of two chiefs. Wolves and buffalo were carved along the sides, and the front was shaped into a majestic eagle's head.

"Don't get in that canoe!" Alex warned.

Cleo looked to the two groups of Plains Indians attending the farewell: Blackfoot and Nez Perce standing side by side. Bloody Chief and Red Wolf looking more like old comrades than bitter war enemies. She looked out to the calm waters of Walloha. They seemed to whisper back, assuring Cleo that she had made the right choice, that all was as it should be.

Cleo stepped into the canoe. Her foot hit the bottom with a dull, hollow thud.

"You don't know these people!" Alex shouted. "Why are you doing this?"

Alex's voice pounded in her skull, but she couldn't explain and she wouldn't stop. She boarded the canoe and sat in silence. She put her hand to her cheek and brushed away a single tear that had escaped from her eye.

"Cleo! Answer me!"

"If they die, we won't remember them," her quiet whisper began. "We won't have their stories to tell. No them . . . no us."

Silence was Alex's only response.

Cleo raised her head. On a hill, far behind the gathering, Eagle perched in a tree. Near the thick trunk stood Badger and Buffalo. Cleo couldn't be sure whether they had come to honor her in a salute to her courage or to make sure she didn't back out.

The three spirits stood as silent monoliths,

voiceless reminders of the importance of Cleo and Seeloo's sacrifice. The Nez Perce and Blackfoot would be saved, and so would the memory of their great gods.

"Seeloo?" Tlesca asked.

Cleo tore her gaze away from the spirits and looked at Tlesca. She smiled at him as he stepped into the canoe and lifted the paddle from her feet.

"You're very quiet," he said, the paddle striking against the water, slicing into Walloha and pushing the canoe out into her watery heart.

"I'm sorry."

"Are you unhappy?"

"No." Cleo paused. She wasn't sure how to answer the question honestly, how to explain to Tlesca that her mood was sadness, but not for what was. It was a sadness for all the days that would never be. "It's so beautiful here," she continued, absorbing every last detail of the landscape. "No wonder they love this lake."

"You're leaving your home; I'm returning to mine. It's a much harder journey for you." Tlesca's words were intended to ease Cleo's soul, but they only struck her as ironic. She knew Tlesca had no idea how hard a journey it would actually be. "But we're at peace and we have each other."

Cleo looked into Tlesca's loving eyes.

"Yes," she said. "We have each other."

Tlesca paddled to the middle of the lake. Walloha's face was flat and calm as a desert. The only sign of movement was the methodical slapping of Tlesca's paddle on the water's surface. For a moment, Cleo wondered if sacrifice did indeed mean death.

"Strange . . . ," Tlesca murmured.

The word hit Cleo like a snowball. She sat erect in the canoe and followed Tlesca's stare to the far edge of the lake. She focused her full attention on the thing that bubbled up from the water. A growing gray mist oozed along the surface and tumbled toward their canoe with a relentless will of its own.

"Walloha." The single word fell from Cleo's mouth and she sank into silence.

The mist widened and spread across the face of Walloha. It rolled toward the canoe and threatened to swallow it whole. Tlesca couldn't avoid the mysterious cloud. He guided them forward. The canoe plunged into the wall of mist and disappeared.

Chapter Nineteen

"Seeloo!" Red Wolf shouted.

"Tlesca!" Bloody Chief called out.

Red Wolf and Bloody Chief immediately raced to the closest canoe and shoved it into the lake, their strongest warriors paddling furiously. They shot toward the mist and their ill-fated children.

"Tlesca!" Cleo cried. The mist was so thick, she could barely see him in the same canoe.

"What?" his voice called out from somewhere in the grayness.

"You'll be all right if you get away from me!" Cleo told him.

"It'll clear . . . ," Tlesca assured her, oblivious to the danger that awaited them. He redoubled his efforts and paddled harder to reach the far shore.

Cleo saw that the mist was not clearing. It was thickening like boiling soup. The air swirled and roiled, and Cleo felt as if she were inhaling cotton with each breath.

"Please! You can swim for it!" Cleo urged Tlesca.

Cleo scampered across the canoe and gripped Tlesca by the shoulders. She shook him, hoping the jolt would make him understand.

"I'm the sacrifice, Tlesca!" she yelled. "My life for peace!"

"What are you talking about, Seeloo?"

"Please! There's no time! You have to swim!"

Far beneath the canoe, glowing particles adhered to each other and took shape. They formed hands and legs and a head. It was Walloha. Her brown eyes looked to the surface far above and she began to rise. The promise had been made. There had been a deal and now it was time to collect. She took no great pleasure in what she was about to do, but what choice did even the goddess of the lake have? In the end, they were all puppets of fate.

"It's the spirit of the lake . . . she wants me, not you!" Cleo's words were painted with fear. They were sharp and panicked. A yellowish glow appeared beneath the canoe and lit the waters around Cleo like a bull's-eye.

"She'll have both of us then!" Tlesca defiantly shouted into the air. "I did not fight for you to lose you now! We are together and we shall always be so!"

"No! Don't say that!" Cleo yelled back. "It's not too late! You can still—"

Walloha reached the surface in an eruption of water. The waves attacked the canoe and upended the craft.

"Cleo!" Alex screamed, helpless to do anything more than watch. Cleo and Tlesca fell into the water, which bubbled and turned like a great pot of boiling stew.

There was splashing and yelling. The mist grew thick as molasses. Tlesca kicked at the water, which seemed to grab at his legs and feet. Water rushed into his mouth. He spit it out and lurched toward the overturned canoe. His hand smacked against the carved wood and he clung to it with all his strength.

"Seeloo!" he cried out. "Seeloo!"

But there was no answer. Cleo had been drawn beneath the water. Tlesca filled his lungs with air and dove beneath the waves of Lake Walloha.

Cleo felt a pull from beneath her, as if the algae below had sprouted fingers and tore at her ankles. She was frightened. Images of her family shot through her head. She would never see them again. What had she done? What had she done?

She drifted through the water, not sure if she was going up or down. The chilled lake stabbed at her limbs, refusing to release her.

In the darkness of the water, Cleo saw a face. It wasn't Tlesca or Alex or her father. It was Walloha, come to claim her sacrifice.

And Cleo remembered. What she had done was create peace. And now it was time to pay that price. Walloha reached out for Cleo. She no longer felt terrified, and she met Walloha with her own hand.

So this is the end? Cleo thought.

Chapter Twenty

Cleo and Tlesca's boat had just overturned. Red Wolf practically leapt into the water himself to follow his daughter.

"Faster!" Bloody Chief screamed to the paddling warriors. "Faster!"

"Seeloo!" Red Wolf yelled.

They reached the overturned canoe as Tlesca dove under the water to search for Cleo. Red Wolf stabbed his war club into the water, extending his arm to its fullest, hoping his daughter would see the mighty weapon.

"Grab the club, Seeloo!" Red Wolf yelled out in vain, as if Cleo's ears weren't filled with water.

There was a splash of water. Red Wolf spotted it. "Over here!" he commanded.

Beneath the water, Cleo embraced Walloha. The fear drained from her body and was replaced by a warm sense of well-being. *This is right,* Cleo reminded herself. She let her limbs go limp and stopped fighting against the spirit of the lake.

In a final show of submission, Cleo slowly let the life-giving air bubble from her lungs. The spheres floated upward through the water and broke the surface, the only evidence Cleo had ever existed.

Back in the study, Alex tore at his hair and paced the room. He pounded his fist against the plasma screen in a fit of explosive frustration.

That was when he saw it.

Red Wolf's war club sliced through the water, extending several feet below the surface of Walloha. Maybe if Cleo reached up, gave one final effort, she could . . .

It's not an animal-tooth saw; it's a war club! Alex thought as he remembered the list of artifacts.

"The war club!" Alex shouted at his sister. "Grab the war club, Cleo!"

Alex's words startled Cleo from her dreamy peace. She saw Walloha's calm eyes staring into her own. She looked upward and there was the war club, mere feet above her head.

The wolf head snaked through the water, Red Wolf blindly waving it in search of his submerged daughter.

Cleo extended her hand. Her fingers wiggled like worms anxiously searching for a way to the mud's surface. Walloha petted Cleo's hair and pressed Cleo's head against her chest. The two slowly sank deeper.

"Come on! Get there!" Alex urged, witnessing the scene.

The teeth of the wolf's-head club flashed from a lone reflection of light and cut through the water to Cleo's eyes. She saw the club and reached out one final time.

There was a flash. Cleo was gone.

Walloha sank to the bottom of the lake, clenching Seeloo in her arms. Seeloo did not fight; she did not resist. This was her decision too; it was her desire to save her people in exchange for her sacrifice. She embraced Walloha as tightly as she embraced her fate, and she disappeared into the water's darkness.

Seeloo was gone.

Chapter Twenty-one

"Cleo!" Alex called out, seeing his sister appear on the study floor.

"Tlesca!" Cleo shouted. She tried to stand, so used to having her legs that she forgot they did not support her in the real world. Once out of the myth, her legs were as useless as a heater in the desert. She collapsed onto her hands and dragged herself toward the plasma screen.

Cleo reached for another Plains Indian artifact that was displayed on the Plasma Screen. Alex grabbed her wrist and stopped her.

"It's okay, Cleo. You're home."

"I gotta go back," she called out. "All those people . . . they'll die if I don't! There won't be peace!"

Alex helped Cleo off the floor and embraced her. It was a hug of relief, the fear that had paralyzed his limbs for the past hours finally leaving his body, but it was also a hug of reassurance to let Cleo know that all was as it should be.

"It's all right," he whispered to her. "You got out in time."

"Seeloo . . . ," Cleo said, raising her weary head from Alex's shoulder. "She's still in there? And Tlesca?"

"Yeah."

The single word soothed Cleo like a warm cup of cocoa. She basked in the glowing consolation that she had helped Seeloo preserve the myth, ensuring that Walloha, Badger, Eagle, Buffalo, and so many others would live in the stories and legends of the Plains Indians.

Cleo collapsed into Alex's arms, finally falling victim to the exhaustion that had devoured every last ounce of her energy.

"Tlesca and Seeloo did drown," Alex told Cleo, referring to his notes. Max had finally gotten back into town and told Alex all he could about Seeloo and her people. The following day, Alex joined Cleo in the cafeteria and filled her in on the history. "It turns out the Blackfoot and the Nez Perce saw the couple's death as punishment for their long war with each other."

Alex looked up. Cleo still stared at her food. She sat, picking at her lunch, leaning on the armrest of her wheelchair.

"Anyway," Alex continued, "they parted as brothers and promised never to fight again. The peace held, Cleo. To this day."

Alex reached out and touched his sister on the shoulder. She smiled at him.

"I thought you'd want to know," Alex concluded.

"Thanks."

Alex wasn't sure what else to say. He could tell that Cleo wanted to be alone. He knew what it was like to come back from an adventure like this, knowing you'd never see those people again, although you'd touched their lives in a profound way. He squeezed his sister's shoulder, stood from the table, and left.

Cleo fiddled with her noodle casserole. It rarely tasted good even on the days she did have an appetite. Her lunch tray gave each food type its own section. Noodles in the middle, vegetables to the left, drink at the top, and a slice of chocolate cake on the right.

A burst of laughter struck Cleo and she searched for its source. It was David, telling a joke to his table of friends.

Cleo knew that she had to let go of Seeloo and Tlesca and claim her own life again.

She grabbed the cake from her tray and rolled over to David's table. She pulled up at the end near David and sat for a moment in silence. All eyes fell on her, unsure what Cleo wanted.

Cleo plunked the chocolate cake in front of David. She tried to stifle her smile, but it broke free in the end.

"For our collision," Cleo informed him.

David nodded in appreciation and allowed himself a tiny smile as well.

Cleo rolled away and let out a tremendous sigh.

That wasn't so hard, she thought, and rolled out to meet the brightness of the noonday sun.

RED WOLF'S DAUGHTER

The legend of Red Wolf's daughter was first written down in the memoirs of the Nez Perce leader Chief Joseph. He remembered it as a story he had heard as a boy. All the retellings of this story can be traced to Chief Joseph's account, although there are different endings depending on the source.

Most versions of the story agree that the Nez Perce warriors traveled to buffalo country every year to hunt the great animals for food. One year, they were attacked by Blackfoot warriors.

The next year, the Nez Perce returned to the buffalo hunting grounds prepared for war, and a great battle raged. Finally the Nez Perce won. But year after year, the fighting continued. Most often, the Nez Perce won.

One year, after winning a great battle, the Nez Perce were on their way home. They hadn't seen any Blackfoot warriors during their journey, so they didn't set any guards before they slept. But the Blackfoot had been following the Nez Perce, and they attacked the sleeping camp, taking a great toll on the unprepared tribe.

The battle raged for days; the Nez Perce grew weaker and weaker as their strongest warriors were killed. It was clear that a Blackfoot victory was imminent, but the sun was setting, so they halted the fighting for the day. The next day, the Blackfoot warriors would decimate the Nez Perce. They returned to their camp for a joyous feast prepared in anticipation of their victory.

Though the Nez Perce warriors faced defeat the next day, they were ready to fight for their honor. But the chief's daughter, a young woman known for her beauty and kindness, could not accept such a harsh end for her people. She slipped out of her village late at night and took her canoe to the Blackfoot camp across the water. She walked directly to the fiercest warrior, who sat at the largest fire.

Though her courage must have been sorely tested, the princess bravely spoke to her fierce opponent. "I am the daughter of the Nez Perce chief, and I have come to speak with you."

She then told the Blackfoot chief that he would find no honor in the battle the next day. Indeed, since all the young warriors had already been killed, he would make war on the old and the helpless. She pleaded with the chief to return to his lands and battle no more.

The chief was not receptive to the young maiden's plea, and he had thrown her to the ground and drawn back his spear when his son stepped in. His son had been moved by the girl's beauty and bravery. He threw his blanket over the girl to protect her.

The chief was finally swayed by his son's arguments, and he agreed to spare the girl, giving her permission to return unharmed to her people.

As she walked to her canoe, the chief's son ran after her. He told her that there was much the two should discuss, and that one night soon she would hear a call—some sources say that of a bird, some say that of a cricket—and she should wait at the edge of the lake for him to appear.

It happened, just as he had said, that several nights later a call came and the chief's son appeared. He had something very important to discuss, and he asked the princess to be his wife.

The girl wanted to know how they could marry while their people warred, and the young warrior assured her that he would convince his tribe to stop if she could convince hers. And so they parted. When they met again some nights later, they were delighted with each other's news—both tribes had consented. Their fathers would meet in several days to discuss the terms of the match, and a lasting peace would come to both of their tribes.

The chiefs did meet and agree to the marriage, and a great wedding feast was held. At the end of the feast, the young couple took their canoe out on the lake. Suddenly, the waters seemed to erupt around them and strong currents seized the canoe, tossing it about violently. The newlyweds fell into the waters and were never seen again, though both of their tribes searched the shore for days.

Sources have two versions of what happened next. One says the Blackfoot tribe felt that the Great Spirit was angry at them for making peace and took their popular chief's son as a price, so they left the Nez Perce lands and returned home, afraid the Spirit would punish them further. But from that day forward, the Nez Perce and Blackfoot tribes were enemies once again.

The other version says that after the deaths of the young people, the two tribes were even more dedicated to peace, saving the Nez Perce from total elimination.